The reason I decided to [illegible] as because my friend Gary F[illegible] I wrote and added a few co[illegible] though I never came from Hilton. Over the years I have had many a drink with guys from Hilton. Back in the seventies Northfield and Hilton didn't get on very well and you couldn't blame them as some numpty from the Council decided to put all Northfield first years to Stockethill School, right in the heart of Hilton. It wasn't that we hated each other, it was just the done thing back in the seventies, and was never very serious they chased us and we chased them. I think it was mostly the Northfielder's from Moir Green that didn't get on with Hilton as us lot from Byron was always fighting with the Mastrick boys.

It was a strange set up back in the sixties and seventies as half of Northfield went to Hilton school and late seventies everyone from Northfield started going to Northfield school. I don't want to come across as an expert on Hilton and I'm only going by some of the stories from people on the growing up in Hilton Facebook page which I set up a few years ago and have enjoyed reading all their comments

HILTON ACADEMY

Hilton an old estate that now forms a residential district of Aberdeen. Hilton is located on a Southwest facing slopes, a quarter -mile Southwest of Woodside and 2 mile northwest of the city centre. The Hilton estate was acquired by the city in the 1920's for housing, with a mix of social housing blocks of that period lying to the north of inter-war bungalows and later development. Quarrying for granite was undertaken here until the 19th century . Hilton house was built in 1729 but demolished in 1926 to make way for Hilton Academy.

The school closed in 1988 and was itself demolished in 1991, having merging with nearby Powis Academy to create St Machar Academy. The site redeveloped for housing in 2000 but the bronze age Lang Stane remains within the grounds. Northern college developed a campus here from 1968, but this was sold off for development following the merger of the college with the University of Aberdeen in 2001.

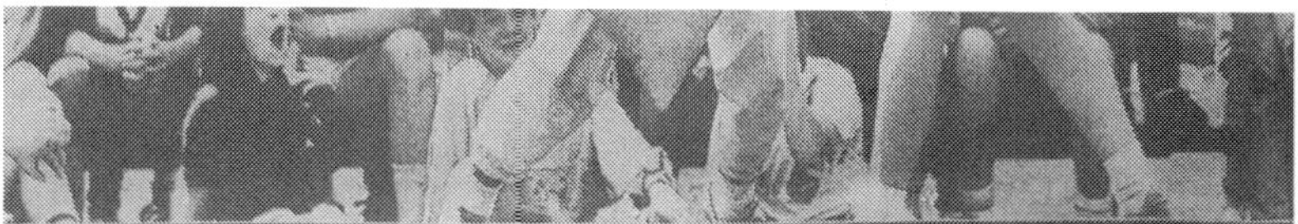

LTON ACADEMY: SIMONE ALL, LEFT, AND TRACY THOMSON BATTLE IT OUT IN A PILLOW FIGHT AT THE SCHOOL'S GALA.

CADEMY: THE LAST OF THE SCHOOL'S PUPILS WAVE GOODBYE IN 1988 AS IT CLOSES ITS DOORS FOR TH

A free standing block of granite, 9 to 10 feet in height , believed to be a bronze age standing stone. It stood in the grounds of Hilton school and may have been moved when the school was built 1949, but if so it was replaced in its original position.

THE TEACHERS

The thing that I thought was funny about the Hilton Facebook group was how all the pupils had nicknames for all of their teachers, us at Northfield only nicknamed about two teachers

Mr CLARK (FROGGY)

GRAHAM RIACH
He smashed the desk lid on the bridge of my nose, blood everywhere, he was as nice as pie to me after my parents went up to see him.

JOYCE WHYTE
Karen Russell I remember he was going to belt you when you had a stookie on your arm, so you walloped him with it when

he was manhandling you.

ELAINE SEWELL

Quite good at throwing chalk or the wooden dusters around and shouting insignificant little pipsqueeks.

ROY THOMSON

He was a psycho.

HAGGIS McDONALD

Getting six of the scud from Froggy Clark, now that was sore.

MR WILSON (PAC MAN)

DARREN REID

We used to call him pac man because of his hand opening and closing just like pac man.

MR MURDOCH (MAD)

DENNIS SCOTT

He would hit a bit of chalk on the table with his belt and crush it, just to show his ego. He was a bit of a weirdo with his little animals in the back room of the class

LESLEY SMITH

He was a bit weird but that's what I liked about him and he made me laugh. One day our class turned the hands on the clock 1 hour fast , so when the 1st period bell went he let us all go thinking it was the end of the 2nd period lesson.

JOYCE TRAIL

I remember Mad Murdoch liked to narrowly miss your hands with his ruler while whacking it hard on the desk.

STEVEN PATTERSON

Mad murdoch he was a bit of a sadist.

MRS NORTON (NIPPY)

AILEEN KEMP

I got the belt from Nippy Norton for not covering my homework book, mind you most of the class got the strap that day.

PETER TAYLOR

I remember when all the boys got the strap from Nippy for causing an uproar, everyone took the punishment until it came to Dougie Wallace, he held out his hand and said to her " if you hit me with that I will grab it from you and take it round your ear" Nippy looked at him and told him just to sit down.

AMANDA HESKETH

Nippy norton she was 5ft nothing with a sharp tongue.

MR ALLAN (DARKIE)

RAY GIBB

Darkie Allan his name put the fear of god into all the P7s going up to Hilton school after the summer break.

DAVID SHARP

He had a fearsome reputation, on our 1st day at Hilton he came onto the stage at our assembley and the kid in front of me was so nervous about him he ended up spewing up.

Apparently him and Mrs Hogarth had a thing going on between them, as they was always together, the whispers and the jokes about this were abundant. Mrs Hogarth she used to sit on the window sill with her legs crossed while telling everyone about hygiene, one day she was caught slithering down the radiator in the English class, and they all thought she had too much sherry at her lunch break.

It looks as though the most likeable Teacher at Hilton was Mr Stroud the art teacher, saddly he passed away last year at the age of sixty six after battling with lung cancer. He loved his music and was in a band in the 70's called Mamalu, he was also known for his vibrant role as the frontman for the city's Jive Bombers an 1980's rhythm and blues band. He had many artistic titles to his name, including winning young Jewellery designer of the year in 1973 when he lived in Edinburgh.

KERRY CHRISTIE

He was the most influential teacher to me, and I will never forget him.

MICHELLE SANGSTER

If it wasn't for this man I would never have become the designer I a'm today. He gave me the heart to love it.

ELAINE McKENZIE

One of the good guys, inspiring in art and brilliant in the Jive Bombers.

GRAHAM HEPBURN

He was a fine gifted teacher and a man who believed in me when other teachers hadn't, I always loved the fact he always called me by my nickname "heppy." It was the little things that made you like and listen to him, such a interesting dude.I managed to get my only A grade at school with his help and never forget him.

CHRIS GRAY

He was one of the best teachers, I really enjoyed my time in the art department, I also remember the time he played at one of our school events and was an amazing singer and Guitarist. He will always be a legend to all the kids he taught.

ROSLYNE ADDISON

The best teacher ever, I loved art because of him, I had him from Primary school and at Hilton, missed hum loads he was a great and kind man.

WAYNE MARNOCK

One of the best and most chilled out blokes.

THE JIVE BOMBERS

MR MORRISON (PEG LEG)

ANDREA ROSS

He used to bob up and down as he was writing on the blackboard, he was a strange one.

STEVEN PATTERSON

Peg leg he taught science, he was once caught snogging the young tech girl in the store room unaware we was all watching from the corridor.

MR DAVIDSON (JOE 90)

DENNIS SCOTT
I remember he had the hots for the German language teacher.

LESLEY ANN GRAY
He was also called Dirty Davidson as he liked the girls but wouldn't hesitate to belt the boys.

MR JACKSON (GHOSTIE)

MARGARET RAE
Sometimes he was called Spike and one day I drenched him with a fire hose. He was the art teacher and would always show us slides about Ancient Egypt, I thought he looked like Boris Karloff.

MR MILNE (CHARLIE FAT HEAD)

GARY FORBES

He was a real bitter man was Charlie fat head and ex headmaster after school dinners he would lock you outside in the pissing rain, howling winds all sorts of shit weather. He would stare out the windows from all quarters of the school, checking doors were locked. He stayed in Cults and when our team was playing at Cults academy he stood on the touchline supporting them. He pulled Terry Cameron into his office on monday morning for elbowing a Cults player on the face.

MARK PRATI

Mr Irving used to send you to Eric's the baker for his rowwies and a ten of cigs.

ELAINE McKENZIE

Remember **Mr Irving** when he first started,he wore pink suit and clogs but was a brilliant teacher and he is still a bit off the wall, even in his sixties

HAGGIS McDONALD

I remember **Mr Kemp** the p.e teacher trying to show us how to correctly lift weights, he bends down and slipped a disc, the class couldn't do anything for laughing as he was yelling out get the nurse get the nurse. Also **Mrs Vatt** trying to give Gogs Milton the strapp, he kept moving his hand away when she tried to belt him, this went on for about ten minutes.

Mr Treasure he was a little hitler. **Miss Drummond** the nurse who would give you paracetamol for every injury going.

MR SPRY (CRISP & DRY)

DONNA EWEN

I got six of the best from Mr Spry in 1981 after getting caught smoking at the dinner hut, boy did u have to dig deep not to scream out and cry, he said to me "Donna thain you will never amount to much"

MARK PRATI

I got the belt from Mr Spry and it really hurt, he was nuts.

PAUL BONNER

Manny Spry had me weeping with six of the scud

WENDY TAYLOR

Great man and a great teacher and he even gave me drum lessons at lunchtime.

GREIG MORRISON

Used to get the scud regular from him and looking back now it was all for some stupid reason. He was a great teacher and the funny thing was after he would give you the scud he would carry on speaking to you normally as nothing had happened.

PETER STEWART

I got a phone call to my office telling me to contact a guy who said it was a private matter. I called back and it was the

Mannie Spry. He said " hey Peter have you heard about this thing on Facebook about Hilton" I had a good laugh with him on the phone, I told him he gets mentioned a lot on the group and he said " what are they saying about me" I told him that most of them thought you was a tit lol. He said that all the places he was a teacher at he always had Hilton in his heart.

DAVE LEE GILES

Brilliant ! He was nearly everyone's favourite! He belted me in my first few weeks at Hilton but I deserved it. I used to love hanging out in his drumming classes and bringing tapes into class. My art skills probably peaked in his class.

JENNIFER MIDDLETON

Really enjoyed Mr Spry's class, he was the only teacher that embraced an error I made and turned it into a positive.

HELEN INNES

Remember he wrote on my report card I had formidable talent ! And when I made a video unit in woodwork he gave me a lift home with it after watching me struggle carrying it.

CRAIG McATEER

A most memorable teacher and memorable for all the correct reasons. Engaging, full of encouragement and willing to spend time to explain things. Great choice of music and I recall a good aim with chalkboard duster.

LAURA BUTLER

Great memories of Mr Spry decorating costumes for the Bon Accord Festival Parade. Also drum lessons at lunchtime.

KEITH CENTERR

Great teacher, called us all by our nicknames, class guy.

LISA MURRAY

Bringing in fake blood capsules that I bought from the Joke Factory and biting into them. Teachers nearly had a heart attack thinking I was bleeding profusely.

KATH BRECHIN

Going under the horse at P.E and moving it when the boys were just about to jump it.

GRAEME HERD

Getting suspended for a month after raising my fist to punch Blinky the science teacher after he took his wooden meter ruler over my knuckles.

JENNY MORRICE

The boys in our history class loosened the projector screen attached to the wall. Mannie mo put the lights off to start the programme, pulled the string and the whole thing came down on his head.

HAGGIS McDONALD

Got sent by Mrs Watt to Froggie Clark to get the scud, she told me to go to room one and tell him she sent me, went to room one and the teacher told me he was in room two, went back up to Mrs Watt and told her Froggie was not in room one. She ended up giving me six of her best, which I would take any time over one of Froggies.

DAVID BUTLER.

We was playing leevio with our mates, Gary Forbes and myself jumped on a bus to Torry while everyone was looking all over Cornhill for us.

DERRY DEANS

Mr Boyce his breath used to stink, one day I let down his tyres on his old rover. Me and Lynn Broon got the scud for throwing an apple at him. **Mrs May** she got her curtains set on fire just like her grub. **Mr Begg** (donald duck) he wore a beany and came to school on his motorbike, dressed in his army coat, gauntlets, and goggles. **Mrs Smith** the headteacher kept her scud in a biscuit tin.

Mr Nicholson science teacher he was a ex major in the para's and was the hardest scudder in school and scared the shit out of me. **Mr Ewing** he used to keep a half bottle of whiskey in his desk drawer. **Mr Smith** he would let us play all kinds of music in his class and always played David Bowie songs. **Mr Donald** kept his bottles of wine in his locker. **Mrs Warnock** who would jump off her chair while giving you the strap. **Mr Baird** the gym teacher with the wig that looked as if it had been through a few cycles in a washine machine.

MRS MONCUR

She was the PE teacher and scared me to death. She was a monstrous looking women, with legs like balloons, I hated her looking into the showers to see if we were all in the cubical (4 to each shower) after our class. She was one evil bitch. Im sure she was a man, she used to make us girls walk around naked in the showers and actually tell us to put our hands by our sides.

SHARON McCUNE

I remember thinking how lucky I was because I wasn't allowed the belt because of my bone disease, **Mr Hughes** the maths teacher who looked like a quaker, was going to give me the belt because I was talking in class, the boys in the class stood in front of me to stop him, while another boy ran to get help from another teacher. A few weeks later he left our school.

MR ALLAN DARKIE

MRS HOGARTH WOODEN TIT

MR FLECK FLECH

MR ARMOUR CATWEASEL

MR JACKSON GHOSTIE

MR EWEN SPINNER

MR PHILIPS GINK

MR CLARK FROGGY

MR MONCUR TUBBY

MISS LOW LOUSY

MRS STEEL METAL MICKEY

MR McBAIN PENGUIN

MRS STRACHAN LADY PENOLOPE

MISS STEWART BUNNY POP

MR FORBES PUPPET HEAD

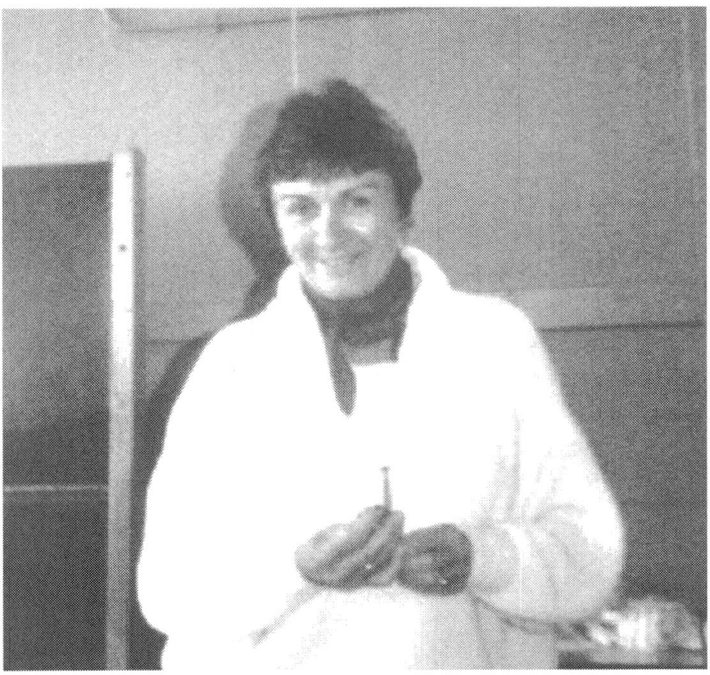

LESLEYANN GRAY

I hated the gym teacher **Mrs Ogston,** she always referred to me as fat girl. Also had to paint a wall in modern studies because I got caught rubbing out catweasel that I had wrote on the wall.

LYN HEWITT

When Aberdeen won the European cup winners cup and we wanted the day off school to go to Union street and Pittodrie to watch them parade the cup, but the school said no!! we marched around the corridors chanting songs. They decided if we wanted the day off we had to get a letter from our parents. Could not believe it when Karen Thomson and myself got to pittodrie and our teacher **Mr Ewen** was in the row behind us.

ADELE WEBSTER

I have met great teachers in my time but none like **Mr Taylor** and heaven help us when he got together with **Mr Spry.** Graham Spry too for letting me skive on Friday afternoons, taking me out in his sports car and generally being a pal when life was shit

Got the belt everyday from **Mr Grant,**he made me put my hand on the radiator before belting me. **Mr Ewen** was a legend of a teacher. Death breath the maths teacher was a right sleaze ball. **Mr Mcbean** was evil he scudded loads of us at Xmas Assembly for taking the piss whilst Feed the World was being played. **Mr Lennox** who was Annie Lennox's uncle and he was a evil fucker.

RONNIE WALKER DUNN

Mr Murdoch I'm sure he kept bees and had a hive at the back off the science class ? There was a hole cut in the glass window that faced onto the car park and can mind the bees flying in and out off it. He also did ESP card tests and tried to teach us how to hang wallpaper.

COLIN BRODIE

One of the boys had a copy of a key that used to let us in to the upstairs balcony of the main Assembly hall. A load of us sneaked into the upstairs part and when **Mr Milne** told everyone to rise at we all stood up from the balcony and you could see the vein on his neck pulse from the balcony.

In my opinion Hilton was one if not the best sporting area in Aberdeen. They produced some amazing football teams and some amazing players. One of the best player to come out of Aberdeen and the most influential was Hilton's John Hewitt. John was a product of Cornhill primary and Middlefield boy's club, and was a schoolboy International before signing for Aberdeen, the club he supported as a boy. He made his full debut for Aberdeen in 1979 at the age of 17, and by 1981 had become a regular in the side. In January 1982 he scored the only goal of the game in a third round Scottish cup tie against Motherwell in 9.6 seconds and the fastest goal recorded in Scottish cup history.

The following season, John again featured prominently for Aberdeen, his two substitute appearances in Europe that he was the Hero. On march 1983 he came off the bench to score the winning goal in the Cup Winners Cup quarter-final tie against Bayern Munich, and then the winner in extra time in the final against the mighty Real Madrid.

John also scored twice in the 1986 Scottish cup final against Hearts. John won three Championship medals, four Scottish cup medals, a Scottish league cup medal, and a European Cup Winners medal, also a UEFA super cup medal with Aberdeen. Something that will never be repeated at Aberdeen again.
In 1989 John moved to Celtic and then four more seasons at ST. Mirren, then a spell as player manager at Dundalk, John retired from the game after a season as assistant manager at Cove Rangers.

It will be a disgrace if this man has not been chosen to have one of the pitches at the new Kingsford Stadium named after him.

Another great player from Hilton school was Ian Wilson. Ian spent one season at Aberdeen but never played a first team game. Ian then signed for Dundee FC for a season. After being freed by Dundee, he then moved to the Highland League club Elgin City. Then in April 1979 Ian got his big break when Leicester City signed him for a record breaking Highland League fee of £20,000. Ian was one of the longest serving Leicester City players and captained the side during a successful eight years at the club. Ian left Leicester City to join Everton FC for a fee of £300,000.

Ian then signed for Istanbul giants Besiktas and in his only season there they won the Turkish League Championship and the Turkish cup.

Ian was capped 5 times for Scotland. In 1993 after leaving Wigan Athletic he became player manager at Peterhead FC for over three years. Ian then moved to Japan to join Nagoya Grampas Eight as assistant manager to his former Leicester City manager Gordon Milne. He then left with Milne to coach his old club Besiktas. After he retired Ian opened his soccer schools in Aberdeen which coaches kids from the age of 4 to 14 year old.

GARY FORBES

Ian Wilson a Hilton Legend and still a great guy.

DON TOWE

Ian "Tickle" Wilson a really nice fella and a terrific player.

DOD MORRISON

John Hewitt, it was a real football fairytale, even more so because it was an Aberdeen loon who delivered the goal that mattered.

GARY BREMNER

I used to play fitba with John and his brother Chub round the back of our flats in Stockethill.

HAGGIS McDONALD

John did Hilton and Aberdeen proud.

DAVID BEVERLEY

John an Aberdeen legend and top bloke. His brother Alan played in goals for our Saturday team, FC Hayloft and was some keeper.

Between 1975-79 Hilton dominated the school football scene. Below are some of the outstanding achievements from the Hilton football teams over the years.

ABERDEEN FC TROPHY 1993 \ 96

ASSOCIATION TROPHY 2000

BOWIE CUP 1994

STEPHEN SHEILD 1989

CHATTAN ROVERS CUP 1992 \ 2008

DICKIE TROPHY 1996 \ 2008

The Hilton Academy team who defeated Harlaw Academy in a Secondary League 1 game today, left to right—back—A. Brebner, W. Robertson, C. Strachan, B. Mackintosh, S. McLaughlin, J. Gilbraith; front—S. Anderson, I. Mathieson, J. Hewitt, K. Walker, K. Whyte.

HANS FYFE TROPHY 1993 \ 2009

WILLIE GIBB TROPHY 1996

TROPHY'S INTER CUP 1997 \ 98 \ 99

DIVISION 1 1995 \ 97 \ 98 \ 99

DIVISION 3 1993 \ 2008

DIVISION 4 1992

DIVISION 5 1991

DIVISION 6 1990

DIVISION 7 1989

GREEN FINAL TROPHY

DENIS LAW TROPHY

SUNDAY WELFARE. LEAGUE & CUPS

TEACHERS FOOTBALL TEAM

Hilton also gad some other sporting achievements In the early years. They had a great Cricket team winning the Aberdeen trophy in 1979. Also in the mid eighties they was one of the top darts team in the city. And they won numerous pool trophys for Murdos bar.

MURDOS POOL TEAM

SCHOOL TRIPS

JOHN DALGARNO

I was on the Baltic cruise when we went to Russia, we took an overnight train to Moscow and there was a raid in the morning because some of the silver spoons went missing.

ANGELA MURRAY

From memory the itinerary was Amsterdam, Oslo, and Copenhagen! I remember the Tivoli gardens and the stink of Indian food in the gallery when we went to eat and feeling sick. Trying to explore at night and the teachers coming in with torches to check on us, and me and another girl jumping into the nearest bed and pretending to sleep and the teachers asking us do we normally sleep together.

HAGGIS McDONALD

We went on a school cruise on the SS Uganda ship and left from the beautiful port of Dundee. We went to Holland, Sweden, and Norway.

NICOLA STUART

I remember going to Paris with Hilton Academy and getting caught buying cider and the teachers ended up drinking it. We left the teacher Joe 90 in the middle of an ice rink and he couldn't get back up. The first night in Paris one of the fifth year guys was out looking for prostitutes and was brought back by the Police.

RAY GIBBS

Our train to Moscow was held up because one of the boys took a Samovar, or maybe just a fancy tea cup, but heaved them out the window when the KJB came onboard, well we thought it was the KJB.

KENNY STRACHAN

When we were travelling by boat to Holland they showed an educational video about Holland, the sea was rough and they did a section on Dutch cheese and all you could see was everyone hanging over the side of the boat being sick.

GONE BUT NEVER FORGOTTEN

JIMMY NICOL

JIM BUCHAN

TERRY MUNRO

PAULINE WALLACE

MARK MILSON

MARTIN MOIR

LEASHY

LYNDA TURNER

DONNA BUTLER GRAHAM PRATT

JOHN LORNIE KIM TOWNEND

R.I.P

THE HILTON TONGS

Even though Hilton was never classed as a violent community like some other rough areas in Aberdeen, they still had there Gang like any other area and was called the Hilton Tongs. A friend of mine from Hilton used to tell me "we are lovers not fighters". I think it was just Northfielder's they were always fighting with, but nothing too serious. But since I started the Hilton Facebook group some of them still have a grudge with Northfielders, but only friendly banter.

LORRAINE SUNLEY

Who remembers jumping on a bus outside school to take you home at dinner time, hoping we would get a fight with the Northfielders.

JENNIFER MIDDLETON

I also remember there was trouble one night after the Groover don't know if it was guys from Powis or Northfield, but they thought they would chase the "Tongs" everyone scarpered, but I believe there had been a plan. A couple of Hilton boys got chased so far up the road but unbeknown chasing them there was a gang of Hiltoner's hiding waiting for them. They must have got the shock of their lives.

DAVE MILTON

Many a fight was had with the Northfield first years coming out of Stockethill.

RICHARD CLUBB

I remember first time I got the school bus! It was at lunch time and it was just after one of the many fights against Northfield (on the big round-about up from Murdo's pub) I decided to sit upstairs, but everyone upstairs was still on a high from the fight. Everyone was jumping around banging on windows etc. the bus driver stopped the bus at the six roads, lets everyone downstairs off the bus and drove the bus straight to the bus Depot. He got out and locked the doors and refused to drive us. We had to wait for another driver to take us back to school to see the Head Teacher.

PETER STEWART

When I was a bus driver many years back, I would speed up from Murdo's bar in order to miss a barrage of kids from Northfield, they hated me, I used to give them the finger on the way back.

THE PUBS, CLUBS, SHOPS, AND PARKS

Many hours of joy and pleasure with the Hilton kids was playing in the Stewart park and the Woodies. In the Woodies was the Rockies where the kids used to climb up and then jump off onto the piles of dead leaves. And as kids the Rockies would have looked like mountains to them. At that time the rumours then was there was a witch burned there, so it was a scary place for the kids them when it got dark.

DENNIS SCOTT

Don't know about a Witch being there but a lot of other weird shit I seen there, but it was probably the glue that did it. lol

JENNY MORRICE

Dinna ken about a witch but there was a wifie we nicknamed Squirrel that stayed beyond the fence. Haven't got a clue how she got the name but she hated us being there in the Woodies. We had a hut and we would hide our stuff there, loads of us including Mandy Ewen, Susan Matson, Dawn Mohoney, Donna Hobson, Julie Forbes, Brian Rait, Ian Locke, Doug Reid, Colin McDougal and we had many a drunking night there.

KIM SUTHERLAND

I mind Jimmer Broon made a zip wire down them, I thought it was really high and loved climbing them. The old shelters we used to climb on them and every school roof around that area.

NEIL BARCLAY

At that age the woodies seemed massive. Full of adventure go back now you realise how small it is was, but the memories are still brilliant.

Before it was Stewart park it was a Quarry. The 4th of June 1894 a Mrs Jean Taylor, who was instrumental in setting up a play area for the children of Woodside. It is a 5 acre site owned by Aberdeen City Council now, which they bought it in 1891, when Woodside was incorporated into Aberdeen, using £500 bequeathed by Mrs Jane Taylor the widow of Mr John Taylor, a merchant in the city. The park was named after a former Lord Provost of the city, Sir David Stewart.

The park contains whale jaw bones presented to the park in 1903 by the captain of the Artic whaler Benbow.

There are five different interpretion in the park, which has been put in place over the years. The project was spearheaded by the Aberdeen Women's Alliance, working in partnership with a number of other groups, including the Aberdeen City Council's unpaid work team, and the Aberdeen Libraries and communications teams.

TAYLORS WELL

The five cairns which are made of recycled granite, dotted around the park, with each bearing information about the green space and surrounding area. One board features information about the Hilton Quarries, which were situated south of Hilton road, while the Northern Quarries were where Stewart Park stands. It also bears information about Isabella Knowles, who had a bad accident which changed her personality completely, leading her to pass herself off as a man and leave her job at the Stoneywood Paper Mills, after which she became a thief, fraudster and jail breaker and escaped from the Aberdeen East jail twice. One cairn tells the story of Margaret Penny, who was the wife of an Aberdeen whaling captain called William Penny.

She went with her husband and son on an expedition to Baffin Island,and it is thought she would have been the first European woman to winter in the Artic Islands, north of Canada.

Other park highlights such as Hilton House recieves its own cairn, where the Aberdeen Women's Alliance spent some time trying to track down inhabitants of the house. They found inez Mary Mackay Ferguson, who lived there with her family until her father – a local solicitor – disappeared, and the family moved to live with other relatives. She went to live with her mother's family in Berkhampstead and became a Suffragist, working with Millicent Fawcett, the leader and founder of the National Union of Suffrage Societies. The final cairn bears the details of tramways in the city, which was built in honourof Mrs Taylor, and the park in the Second World War.

During the Aberdeen Blitz of April 21 1943, three 500-kilo high explosive bombs were detonated in Stewart Park. One killed a young man who was walking through the park with his girlfriend, who was seriously injured.

FRED MUNRO

No witch, but we burned many bonfires in winter Friday nights to keep warm while getting pissed.

TERASA CONNER

I fell off the swing and knocked the wind out of myself, then at night when it was pitch dark we would scare the living daylights out of each other.

MICHELE PETER

You could climb the easy of hard sides of the rockie's. The ropey was great fun and spent many hours playing there and when slightly older, used to be the place to drink our mixies or cider.

LYNNE GOW

I remember when we used to go on the ropey swing and jennfer middleton banged against the rocks and broke her thumb.

JENNIFER MIDDLETON

My thumb got stuck between the stick and the rope, so I was hanging by my thumb, also still have the scar on my leg where I bounced off the rocks.

KEITH PERFECT

What happened in the woodies stays in the woodies lol.

COUTSIE'S FARM

Coutsie's farm was a very popular place for the kids, it was mostly waste land behind the Ambulance station. A lot of the kids went down there to collect birds eggs or see the horses. There was some plots there and the kids used to go down and steal pea pods and sell them.

JOHN DALGARNO

I remember coutsie's , we used to go down there quite often, although mainly to find birds eggs! I remember the farmer chased uss of his land a few times, one time we jumped the barbed wire fence and one of my mates ended up with stitches. We used to carve our names on the trees, also sometimes we would go in by the ambulance garage for a cup of soup out of the machine.

IAN PRATT

I remember the great days at the Golden Cairns. The first day I walked in there. my best friend Jim Kerr and myself drank in Murdo's all the time, and one day decided to try the Cairns out! Talk about a life change for me, spent the best days of my life in there.

ALAN MOIR

I remember when the Cairns was actually being built, my cousin and myself were doing what kids did back then on building sites. We were inside when security, builders and Police turned up and we had no way out. My cousin promptly put his butt through a newly installed window and we got away scott free.

CAMERON WELCH

I remember the hairdressers in the Arcade opposite Massey's we used to call the wifie that ran it " scissors happy" she would be cutting your hair and smoking a fag at the same time. Also the Librarian in the library with this huge mole on her face with hairs growing out of it.

Other places the kids would hang out was the Rosehill shops and some nights at the church at the bottom of Rosehill drive which would have a disco on a Saturday night and it was called the Hilton Groover. Across the road from there was an old haunted house that was empty for years, and the kids stayed well away from it.

HAZEL JONES

I remember going to that church at the Saturday night disco, nowhere to sit, so you would just walk around in circles if you wasn't dancing. The last record played at night was Let's get together again by the Glitter Band.

CORNHILL PRIMARY SCHOOL

Cornhill primary school was built in the 1950s and is situated at Cornhill Drive. It was basically pedestrianised from the far end of Stockethill to the bottom of the Cornhill field... apart from Foresterhill, and the reason was a young boy called Paul Whyte was knocked down by a truck outside the school and his leg was badly injured in the early Seventies. I think it is such a shame that all the great football teams and football players that came out of there, and now they have banned the children from playing football in the playground.

ROSEHILL SHOPS

The shops in Rosehill were there in 1964 till the 70s, you had the TSB, Harry's Paper shop, the Butcher shop owned at first by Alex Goldie then Jim McKenzie, ma and pa's chip shop,

Harry's grocer shop and a builders next door. Harry's had to close at school lunchtime after he got caught selling cigarettes to under age kids. The owner Harry Bremner used to get such a bad time from the kids, they called him Harry Half Pence. and his windows always got pelted with snow balls. He used to keep his sweets behind a glass cabinet as he knew the kids would have robbed him blind, he would sell you a fag in a bag for 10p.

HAGGIS McDONALD

I did a Sunday paper round for him, and had two bags of papers and got 50p for the pleasure and spent most of it in his shop, he was a cunning old so and so. I used to buy smoking Kenny's from Harry and smoked them in the woodies.

SHERRY THOMSON

Harry wasn't as green as his cabbage looking, he knew the right side of a 10p the grippy git.

LYNNE CRAIGMYLE

I worked in Harry's when I was 13 and getting a whole 90p an hour.

MIKE COURAGE

Jim McKenzie the butcher did a rare potted heed. Visual video shop and Arcade games right next door and Harry jew bag Newsagent.

KENNY BURNS

lost count of the number of times I got dragged out of the ABC Visual by my mum.

PAULINE ANDERSON

harry bremner owned all the shops and leased them out. There was the butcher then his grocery shop then ma and pa's chipper. Then the barbers come paper shop. And finely the tsb bank later. The barber come paper shop became abc taxis which was run by jim lawrie the golfers paul lawries father. Harry had a nickname for those he was fond of. I worked in his shop and delivered newspapers for him. Not everyone could take his humour. But he was a great man.

NEIL BARCLAY

I mind the video shop I used to sell pirate videos for the guy that worked there for 50p a video, gutted when it shut.

Hiltons main pub is Murdo's bar, which was built in 1972 and owned by Murdos Bruce. Back in the seventies and eighties it was a no go area for Northfielders, but how things change as people from all areas drink there now, and is one of the busiest local pubs in Aberdeen.

They even had an International pop star David Bowie going in for a pint. When Murdo's closed at 2.30 and opened again at 5.00, Bowie came in a couple of times during the closed hours for a drink with Murdo Bruce's daughter. Bowie's son was looked after by his nanny Marion Skene who lived in Cornhill Court.

CORA GALLEY

Marion Skene used to collect him from school and take him to Cornhill Court for the holidays, they used to call him Joe. Marion passed away at David Bowies Switzerland home last year. Bowie even left her money in his will.

DAVE LEE JONES

Cool just imagining Bowie buying a Green final. Does this mean there is a fair chance that bowie himself might have heard of the Tongs, Gothenburg and how minky **Northfield Sensibles** were !?

QUOTES FROM THE HILTON

FACEBOOK GROUP

SHERRY THOMSON

Walking up to the chipper singing Shout by lulu, wearing my Pork pie hat, Oddball jeans, Y Cardigan and Adidas kicks. We thought we were archie! Lol.

GARY FORBES

It's really strange, my daughters stay in Cornhill and Rosehill but it's all more or less a new breed of neighbors/ people. It's great to have brilliant memories of all your pals mums and dads houses as you pass them. I've been in Rosehill 20 years, before that Stockethill 10 years after being brought up in Cornhill. I'll never leave my beloved Hilton area now, my kids are the same as me I think. I know people move on to pastures new but it's still a great feeling waking up in this area and speaking to your old pals. It's amazing how some people just disappear of the face of the earth right after you leave school. Some terrific photos and memories on this page. Also never forget our special Hilton pals who are no longer with us.
Karen boag I'm the same Gary. Brought up in Cornhill, stayed in Stockethill, moved out of the area for five years and hated every minute. Back at Stockethill now and back in my childhood home.

RAY THOMSON

Playing football in Stewart Park, I hid behind a tree the keeper (Peter Stewart) came out with the ball, I sneaked up behind him took the ball and scored, he went mental.

BILL STUART

Unscrewing the lid of the wood glue, Mr Lennox was showing us stuff and didn't realise the lid was not on properly, glue went everywhere and the whole class was kept back after school. Nobody owned up to it either. **Stick** together us Hiltoner's.

ALISTAIR STEWART

Hilton school my pal Walter Simple, yes that was his real name had a live 22 bullet and after class was empty we stuffed the key hole with putty and put the bullet in the middle. Next morning waiting for the teacher to open up the class and he couldn't get in so he went away to the woodwork class and came back with a hammer and a centre punch, well he started to hit the putty and we had to stop him and say what we had done. We got six of the best for that one.

KEVIN MASSON

Going to be honest and say I didn't like school very much, probably because I wasn't very good. Remember having a cig round the side of the science block, my walk to school took ages up past the Stewart Park and past the Rockies. Many a fight took place in the Stewart Park.

PAUL MILNE

My memory was getting threatened by the Woodside mods whilst walking up from the Hilton Groover to the chip shop. I had the "honour" or was made to dance to Gary Numan's Are Friends Electric I never had a choice.

GARY FORBES
TRIBUTE PAGES

It is with great sadness that while in the process of writing this book that Gary Forbes had passed away. When Gary told me he wasn't in the best of health and also myself not in the greatest of health decided to put the book aside until a later date. When Gary told me he was on the mend we decided to crack on with the book even against some stumbling blocks. But I was gutted not to get the book out in time to show Gary before he passed away. So this book will be dedicated to a Gary who in my eyes was **Mr Hilton.** A legend and well loved by not just Hilton but Northfielders and all over Aberdeen.

DAVID MERCHANT

One of the best years as a footballer was spent under the man that we lost today he was a proper manager, a manager that knew how to treat his players and shown you the utmost respect. Known Gary from as young as I can remember and he is a guy who always had time for you, wouldn't walk past without speaking to you and asking about how your life was going. Never beat him at pool no matter how hard I tried. A guy that will be missed by everyone who came into contact with him.

DENISE SUTHERLAND

Gary it was an absolute honour and privilege to have known you, you were an absolute gem of a guy and you will have left many people broken-hearted, not only in Aberdeen but in many places as you knew everyone and will have made an impact on loads of peoples lives. I also would like to thank you for speaking at Billy Smith's funeral of which you did him proud and the story about the chinos will live with me forever.

MELANIE McDONALD

I feel privileged to have known such an all round top bloke, a true gent, who will be missed by so many not least of all his family whom he adored.

CRAIG FRASER

Gary signed me for Glentaner juniors from Hilton under 19s when I was only 18 and it was the best team I have ever played for. He then tried to sign me when he moved to Ellon which I was gutted when it didn't happen. There wasn't a second thought for me, when he called me about the Hilton amateur side he was setting up and if I wanted to be part of it. I spent the best part of my football career playing for this man and he certainly knew how to get the best from his players. We had so much success in the seven years I played for him with numerous cup and league wins. He was a true winner and inspiration to so many young footballers.

SARA WALKER

He was one in a million. A true gentleman. They defo broke the mould when they made our Gary. I will never forget our Monday night piss ups in Murdos, you had an absolute heart of gold, and always seen the best in all of us.

DEREK HENDERSON

A very good friend of a number of years, absolute gentleman. You meet certain people over a lifetime that strikes a cord and you respect, Gary was one of them, he just needed to walk into a room and the whole room lit up. And what you did with the Hilton team was an amazing achievement. Top bloke your legacy will live on.

JEFF SMITH

I was lucky enough to meet Gary back in 2013 when he took the reigns of the Murdos pool team. He took us to the top, we won everything. Gary was a true competitor and ruthless in victory which stemmed back from his Hilton football days. And never forget the time you bought that bloody tank.

GRAHAM HEPBURN

The area of Hilton and Murdos has lost it's Godfather. I remember growing up in the area and one of the first time I seen Gary, he was training his beloved Hilton FC with his sidekick Jimmy Nicholl, I was in awe of the both of them.

TESSA FORBES

Everything I have ever achieved so far in life, everything I have in my life and everything I have worked hard for, all of my dreams, everywhere I have been and places I still want to go, things I want to do, my yolo lifestyle, my temper, strong mind, positive attitude, determination and fight, my amazing close family. Everything comes down to my dad he could not have done a better job with our family and we are forever grateful to have such a great and respected man.

NINA FORBES

Although there is a massive emptiness now, it is not the end. Legends live forever and dad Gary will be with all of us in our heavy hearts and fond memories forever and always.

MIKE SHERAN

All this wonderful comments from Gary's friends say it all about what a true gentleman he was, and the post below which Gary posted on the Facebook group will touch us all.

GARY FORBES

Thank you wonderful Hilton people. This has been an emotional night for lots of us. I am going to ask my pal Michael Sheran when he writes his book about Hilton, if he can dedicate a chapter or two, to our dearest who are not here any more with us. We want them to know they will never ever be forgotten and their memories will be in a book for generations to read and keep.

MR HILTON
R.I.P

Printed in Poland
by Amazon Fulfillment
Poland Sp. z o.o., Wrocław

51578139R00040